THE THREE BEARS

ILLUSTRATED BY

F. Rojankovsky

A GOLDEN BOOK • NEW YORK

Western Publishing Company, Inc., Racine, Wisconsin 53404

This is one of the Little Golden Books which bring children the best of the world's folk tales with fresh illustrations by outstanding children's book artists. Feodor Rojankovsky's pictures for books published in this country and in Europe have endeared him to children the world over.

Once upon a time there were three bears—
a great big papa bear, a middle-sized mama
bear, and a wee little baby bear.

They lived in a little house in the forest.

And they had three chairs—a great big chair for the papa bear, a middle-sized chair for the mama bear, and a wee little chair for the baby bear.

And upstairs there were three beds—a great big bed for the papa bear, a middle-sized bed for the mama bear, and a wee little bed for the baby bear.

One morning the mama bear made some
porridge for breakfast.

She filled a great big bowl for the papa bear, a middle-sized bowl for the mama bear, and a wee little bowl for the baby bear.

But the porridge was too hot to eat, so the
three bears went out for a walk in the forest.

That same morning a little girl called Goldilocks was walking through the woods.

She came to the three bears' house. And she
knocked on the door, but nobody called, "Come
in." So she opened the door and went in.

Goldilocks saw the three chairs. She sat in
the great big chair. It was too hard. The middle-
sized chair was too soft. The baby chair was just
right—but it broke when she sat on it.

Now Goldilocks spied the porridge.
"I am hungry," she said.
So she tasted the porridge.
The porridge in the big bowl was too hot.

The porridge in the middle-sized bowl was too cold. The porridge in the wee little bowl was just right—so she ate it all up.

Then Goldilocks went upstairs and tried the beds.

The great big bed was too hard.
The middle-sized bed was too soft.

But the wee little bed was oh, so nice! So Goldilocks lay down and went to sleep.

Then home through the forest and back to
their house came the three bears—the great big
bear, the middle-sized bear, and the wee little
baby bear.

The moment they stepped into the house,
they saw that someone had been there.

"Humph!" said the papa bear in his great big
voice. "Someone has been sitting in my chair!"

"Land sakes!" said the mama bear in her middle-sized voice. "Someone has been sitting in *my* chair."

"Oh dear!" cried the baby bear in his wee little voice. "Someone has been sitting in *my* chair, and has broken it all to bits."

Then they all looked at the table.

"Humph," said the papa bear in his great

big voice. "Someone has been tasting my porridge."

"And someone has been tasting *my* porridge," said the mama bear.

"Someone has eaten *my* porridge all up,"
said the baby bear sadly.

Then up the stairs went the three bears, with

a thump thump thump,
and a trot trot trot, and a skippity-skip-skip.
(That was the wee little tiny bear.)

"Humph," said the papa bear in his great big voice. "Someone has been sleeping in my bed!"

"And someone has been sleeping in *my* bed," said the mama bear.

"Oh, dear!" cried the baby bear in his wee little voice. "And someone has been sleeping in *my* bed, and here she is right now!"

Goldilocks opened her eyes and she saw the
three bears.

"Oh!" said Goldilocks.

She was so surprised that she jumped right
out of the window and she ran all the way home.
And she never saw the house in the forest again.